The
Little Wooden
Swing Set

DARLENE LOVEN

To order additional copies of this book, contact:
Xlibris
844-714-8691
www.Xlibris.com
Orders@Xlibris.com

ISBN: Softcover   978-1-6698-1137-4
         Hardcover   978-1-6698-1138-1
         EBook   978-1-6698-1136-7
    Library of Congress Control Number: 2022901809
         Print information available on the last page

Rev. date: 02/11/2022

The Little Wooden Swing Set

Fred and I are driving through the countryside, looking for deer while singing songs, chatting and laughing. The car windows are down because the sun is shining, and it is a beautiful day. The air is filled with the smells of summer and new mown grass. I guess we were making too much noise to see any wildlife except for squirrels, even in our favorite park. We sit in the park enjoying our ice cream cones and then try another road with the hope of seeing deer and new fawns. Suddenly up ahead I spot a wooden swing set perched on the side of the road with a "For Sale" sign attached. Why was it for sale? Is it sturdy? Would it be a fun thing to add to our yard? Can it be taken apart and moved easily? It may be too much work for Grandpa.

I suggest to Fred that we stop and check it out. "My granddaughter would sure enjoy these swings when she comes to visit!" I can imagine the good times we would have swinging and singing silly songs in time to the forward and back movement of the swings.

A phone number was attached to the swing set. I wrote it down on a napkin we had in the car from the ice cream cones Fred and I had for treats while touring the parks and lakes. It was very nice of the lady at the ice cream shop to give us those extra napkins. Perhaps she knew Fred would be messy as he slowly savored every single slurp of that chocolate cone. She was correct!

Fred and I drove back to his apartment for his coffee time with the residence of his assisted living apartment, then I raced home (but not too fast!) to tell Ellie about it. She was staying with us for a few days while her mom and dad enjoyed a little holiday. We asked Grandpa if he thought it might be a good idea to purchase it for her visits. We really need Grandpa to say "yes" because he would be doing the heavy work to bring it back to our house! "Yes, yes!", say Ellie and Grandpa.

"We should call the phone number right away to make sure the swings are still there," said Ellie. We are very happy to find that they are! Quickly we hop into Grandpa's truck to drive through the countryside again, but we need to drive slowly because Ellie is certain that we have pumas in our midst, and we hunt them each time we drive anywhere! We never see any, but we are always searching for one that might be lurking on the side of the road or in the woods or maybe even enjoying a drink of water from the lakes or ponds.

Grandpa teases Ellie and me that we may not find the swing set because her Granny is not very good at keeping directions. I scowl at Grandpa and point up the road excitedly. "There it is! It's still here, just waiting for us to take home for you to swing high, up to the sky!" Grandpa is very good at taking things apart and putting them back together so, in no time at all, we are headed back to our house with a swing set, checking for pumas all the way! "I wonder if we will ever see a puma, Grandma," says Ellie. "We just need to keep looking, I guess, and be patient. If there are any pumas around, we should see one!", I say.

Now, where should we set up the swings? It would be nice to have a bit of shade so we decide next to the woods may be the very best spot. Grandpa works so hard putting the swing set back together! One set of legs had to be removed for it to fit into the box of Grandpa's pickup so first job was to reattach those. "I'm so excited! I'm going to swing high into the sky and never come down till the 4th of July!", says Ellie. And she did! She would swing every chance she got.

But then we got so much rain. The mosquitoes were fierce and very hungry! Any time Ellie went to the edge of the woods to play On her swings, those mosquitoes would attack her. Grandpa and I decided it should be moved to a sunnier spot, so we loaded it on the trailer for him to move to the sunny back yard. "This is much better! Now I can swing high up to the sky and not get itchy from the mosquitoes!" And so, she did!

As Ellie got older, she wasn't as interested in swinging as she was in rollerblading and swimming, horseback riding and competitions, even piano lessons for a few years. Josh, her cousin, is much younger and loves to swing especially if Ellie is with him. My how they enjoyed times together on that swing set, giggling as Ellie pretends to fall over when Josh's feet got close to her. So much fun! Josh had a baby swing at first, but soon grew and wanted to learn how to pump his legs and swing on his own. Ellie, along with Josh's mommy soon had him pumping on his own and swinging high in the sky just like Ellie.

Josh soon outgrew the swing set, as Ellie had before him, and moved on to rollerblades, bike riding, Legos, learning to hunt ducks, fishing and baseball.

The swing set looked lonely waiting for a little one to swing high up in the sky just like Ellie and Josh did. I wondered what we should do with it. There must be someone who would love it as much as Ellie and Josh did. But it was not a fancy swing set. It had no slide, no colorful horse or glider; just two swings and a trapeze bar. Not nearly as newfangled as the playground equipment at the park with tunnels and jungle gyms and teeter-totters!

Maybe we could put it on the side of our road and hope for another grandma and grandpa to see it and take it home for their grandkids. We put a :"FREE" sign on it, hoping for a grandparent to see the swings and imagine the fun memories they would share with their grandkids. There are many more memories to be made, I am certain!

Suddenly a car appeared to slowly drive by the little swing set! Is it another granny looking at the "FREE" sign? Is she imagining her grandchildren playing on the swings and swinging high up to the sky? Oh, I hope so! But no, the car just drove by without stopping. Maybe she needs to talk to her husband about it like I did with mine. Maybe she was trying to figure out if she could get it home. Oh, how I hope she returns! I just know there are many more days of laughter and fun to be had on this swing set!

Another hour went by before the lady in the blue car drove slowly down the road, examining our little swing set. Will she stop? Will she like it? Does she have little children who would enjoy swinging high in the sky or maybe she's a grandma too and can imagine the fun her grandkids would have on the old wooden swing set. Oh, I hope she stops! Up to the end of the road and back again, she drove, finally stopping to get a better look. She said, "Are you really giving this swing set away? It looks perfect for our grandchildren to play on while they visit us at the farm! They would love it!" I told her she was welcome to take it, that we were hoping it could go to another grandpa and grandma to share with their grandkids. She had to ask her husband if they could get it safely to the farm and did he think their grandkids would enjoy playing on it. The very next morning they came with a trailer and loaded the swings.

Now that little swing set is sitting in the shade at another grandpa and grandma's house, being enjoyed by their grandchildren! And maybe they are flying" high up to the sky" just like Ellie and Josh did. Oh, I hope so!